THE GOLDEN SLIPPER

Library of Congress Cataloging-in-Publication Data

Lum, Darrell H. Y.
    The golden slipper: a Vietnamese legend / written & adapted by
Darrell Lum; illustrated by Makiko Nagano.
        p.   cm. — (Legends of the world)
    Summary: A variation on the Cinderella story, in which a kind-hearted
young woman meets her prince with the help of animals she has
befriended.
        ISBN 0-8167-3405-4 (lib. bdg.)   ISBN 0-8167-3406-2 (pbk.)
        [1. Folklore—Vietnam.]   I. Nagano, Makiko, ill.   II. Title.
    III. Series.
        PZ8.1.L969Go   1994
        [398.21]—dc20   93-33588

Printed in the United States of America.

10 9 8 7 6 5 4 3 2 1

Anhdo

THE
GOLDEN SLIPPER

A VIETNAMESE LEGEND

RETOLD BY DARRELL LUM   ILLUSTRATED BY MAKIKO NAGANO

TROLL ASSOCIATES

mong the foothills along the Red River in Vietnam, a poor rice farmer lived with his beloved daughter, Tam. The farmer's wife had died, and when he remarried, his new wife treated Tam cruelly. She would often beat the girl or send her to bed without any dinner.

After the birth of her own baby girl, the new wife's neglect of Tam became worse. The new daughter, Cam, was cherished as much as Tam was despised. In time the farmer grew weak at the thought of his dear daughter's mistreatment until, at last, he died of a broken heart.

Tam missed her father's kind laughter. Now in the care of her wicked stepmother, Tam worked in the rice fields all day and did all the household chores at night, sleeping for just a few hours in a dirty corner of the kitchen.

Often, she would dream herself away from her surroundings and imagine herself to be a beautiful princess, married to the prince and living in the royal household. But Tam had little hope of marrying a prince, or marrying anyone for that matter. What little money the family had was saved for Cam's dowry.

Once Tam complained, "Stepmother, why must I work in the fields all day and do all the housework, too?"

"Spoiled girl!" her stepmother replied. "Now that your father is gone, who else will work in the fields? Your sister is too young and too frail to work." And with that Stepmother and Cam laughed and whispered to each other.

One afternoon, Cam announced, "Mother, Tam and I will catch prawns from the pond for our dinner. Will you cook them for us?" Stepmother agreed, and the girls went to catch the freshwater shrimp.

Tam quickly filled her basket with prawns. She knew to stand quietly in the water and watch for the slight movements of the prawns among the rocks. Then she swept her net swiftly through the water to catch them.

Cam on the other hand, spent the afternoon playing in the trees. She was afraid to step into the water for fear of getting her long skirt wet. By late afternoon, she realized that she had no prawns to bring home. Spotting a lotus flower across the pond, she begged Tam, "Older sister, before we go, please pick that pretty flower for me. You will bring home the prawns but at least I will bring home a flower."

Tam waded across the pond to pick the flower. But when she returned, her basket was empty and Cam was gone. Tam sat next to her basket and cried. She missed her father more than ever and wished that her real mother were alive to hold and comfort her.

am's tears made the surface of the pond shimmer. She heard her name being called in a soft voice. Tam looked up and saw a beautiful woman dressed in the royal colors, golden yellow and deep orange, standing before her.

"A princess should not be crying," said the woman.

"I am not a princess. Look at me!" Tam cried, pointing at her ragged clothes and her empty basket.

"You are a princess," the woman replied. "You are strong and kind and you have a gentle heart. Listen to the animals that surround you. Listen with your heart and everything around you will take care of you." With that, the woman vanished. But in Tam's basket, a small catfish swam, its scales of golden yellow and deep orange shimmering in the afternoon sunlight. Tam hurried home and set the fish free in a nearby pond.

Each night after dinner, Tam slipped out to the pond to feed her fish with food she had saved from her bowl. For indeed, Tam had a gentle heart and all the creatures of the earth were her friends.

Each morning, Tam was awakened by the crowing rooster. When she went out to feed it, she said, "Here you are, my morning friend. You need some breakfast since you start your day so early." Then she tossed the rice from her own bowl to the rooster. Tam noticed the golden yellow and deep orange feathers on the bird. "You must be a royal rooster," she teased. "You have the colors of the Emperor's robes."

The rooster hungrily scratched and pecked each grain of rice. Then it scratched again, as if asking for more. "I have no more rice, my friend," Tam scolded gently.

The old horse also seemed hungry as it pulled its cart slowly out to the fields each day. Tam allowed the horse to stop frequently to chew on the grass along the way. She said, "I know you are tired, Old Horse. Once the harvest is done, you will have a rest and a bucket of grain. I promise." The horse's coat, covered with dew, shone golden yellow and orange as it slowly pulled each cartful of rice plants from the fields.

Tam looked up into the sunlight and remembered that it would soon be time for the Autumn Festival, when farmers celebrated their harvest and the prince paid a visit to the village. The farmers made offerings to the gods to thank them for their harvest. And for a few days the work in the fields was forgotten and the villagers celebrated.

While Tam worked in the fields, Cam could only think about the new clothes that Stepmother had promised her for the festival. "I will have a silk blouse this year and long, flowing pants," she chattered. "The prince will surely see me in the crowd and choose me to be his princess. Then I will wear only the royal colors, golden orange and yellow."

Tam, too, had dreams of brand-new clothes and of marrying the prince. She wished that the words of the mysterious woman were true. But all she could hear was Cam's taunt, "What are you going to wear to the festival, Tam?"

On the day of the Autumn Festival, Stepmother pointed to the cartful of rice plants and said to Tam, "You may go to the festival when you have finished husking all the rice in this cart. I promised the tailor a bag of rice if he would sew Cam's outfit."

Tam watched as Cam prepared for the festival in just the outfit she had hoped for: a silk blouse and long, flowing trousers. "Doesn't she look beautiful, Tam?" Stepmother asked as they left for the festival.

Tam turned away. Through her tears, the sunlight shimmered off the mountain of rice plants. It would take many days to complete the task that Stepmother had set before her.

Just then, Tam looked up to see the mysterious woman. "Husking is much more fun when you have friends to help," the woman said. Suddenly a flock of ricebirds swooped down on the cart to husk the rice. They shook each plant until all the grains fell into a pile at Tam's feet.

Then the birds fluttered their wings in the mountain of rice and a cloud of hulls flew up. Tam closed her eyes against the dust and the wind. When she opened them, the hulls were gone and, in their place was a light yellow silk blouse. Tam slipped on the blouse and ran to the pond to look at her reflection. As Tam's catfish came out to admire her, its tail splashed a light rain of water on her tattered trousers. Tam looked down and saw that her rags had turned into a pair of flowing, black trousers.

Tam's friend, the rooster, was now crowing loudly. "Princess Tam! Princess Tam!" it seemed to say. The rooster bowed and scratched at the dirt at her feet. Tam laughed and bowed. "Emperor Rooster, how do you think I look?"

The rooster continued to scratch at the hard dirt until the edge of a beautiful pair of golden brocade slippers peeked through the ground. Tam slipped them on. They completed an outfit that only royalty would wear.

When Tam returned to the house, Old Horse stood snorting and impatiently pawing the ground. Its coat was glistening and smooth, and the horse had a new leather bridle and jeweled saddle. Tam exclaimed, "Old Horse! You are beautiful!"

The mysterious woman held the reins and helped Tam into the saddle. "You are truly a princess," she said.

Old Horse trotted slowly at first, then broke into a gallop as it neared the royal household. Tam could only hold on. As they rushed toward the festival grounds, one of Tam's slippers fell from her foot. "Wait," she cried, but the horse would not stop.

ater, as the prince and his court left for the festival, a soldier spotted Tam's fallen slipper. He gave it to the prince, who had never seen such a beautiful work of art.

Word spread quickly through the crowd that the prince wished to meet the owner of the brocade slipper. First, the ladies of the court had to try on the slipper. Next, all the noblewomen tried. At last, any woman at the festival was invited to try her foot in the slipper. And although it appeared that the slipper would fit many women, no one could slip it on.

Stepmother pushed Cam to the front of the line, convinced that Cam's foot would fit. She was already dreaming of her life at court as the mother of the princess. As Cam struggled, Stepmother shouted, "Try it again! You're not trying hard enough!"

Amidst the commotion, Tam's horse gently nosed its way forward. People backed away when they saw the beautiful young maiden dressed in royal colors. As Tam held out her foot to the prince, Stepmother watched in disbelief. The beautiful brocade slipper fit Tam's foot perfectly!

The prince promptly fell in love with Tam and promised to make her his bride. As Tam and the prince rode away, Stepmother shouted, "She is my daughter! She is my daughter!" But the people just pointed at Stepmother and laughed. "Foolish old woman!" they said.

Even after Tam and the prince were married, Stepmother could not forget the laughter that day at the Autumn Festival. She spent many days after that scolding Cam. "Why didn't your foot fit the slipper?" she would shout.

Occasionally, in the quiet of evening, Stepmother would hear a strange sound around the house. It might have been the splashing of a catfish, the crowing of a rooster, or the whinny of a horse. Or it might have been the sound of laughter coming from the prince and his new bride.

30

The tale of *The Golden Slipper* comes from Vietnam, where the story is also called *The Brocade Slipper.* Like a number of other countries in Asia, Vietnam has been shaped and influenced by the invasions of armies from other countries. At one point in its history, Vietnam was ruled for a thousand-year period by the Chinese, who called the country *Nam Viet.* The presence of other powers in Vietnam is not just a thing of the past, though; it has occurred in this century as well.

The land of Vietnam is predominantly mountainous, but it has two major lowland river systems: the Red River in the north and the Mekong River in the south. The monsoon, or rainy, season can bring as much as eighty inches (200 cm) of rainfall per year. This level of rainfall, along with warm temperatures, makes Vietnam very suitable for the production of rice, coffee, tea, and spices.

Many cultures throughout the world have stories like *The Golden Slipper.* For instance, a similar tale that arose in Europe is *Cinderella.* Under China's rule of Vietnam, a small number of powerful families ruled over a much larger number of poor families. It's not difficult to see why a story such as *The Golden Slipper* became popular, telling as it does of poor girls dreaming about prosperous lives with powerful princes.